D0607136

BY THE LIGHT OF THE CAPTURED MOON

by Julian Scheer *illustrated by* Ronald Himler

HOLIDAY HOUSE / NEW YORK

Printed in the United States of America
The text face is William Morris' Golden type.
The medium of the artwork is watercolor
and gouache over pencil.
www.holidayhouse.com
First Edition

Library of Congress Cataloging-in-Publication Data

Scheer, Julian.
By the light of the captured moon / by Julian Scheer ; illustrated by Ronald Himler.—1st ed.
p. cm.
Summary: The night before school starts,
Billy tries to hold onto the fun he and his friends have been having
by capturing the last full moon of summer and trying to hide it in his bedroom.
ISBN: 0-8234-1624-0 (hardcover)
[1. Moon—Fiction. 2. Summer—Fiction. 3. Friendship—Fiction.]
I. Himler, Ronald, ill. II. Title.

PZ7.S3424 By 2001
[E]—dc21
00-044876

For Sue and Hilary
J. S.

To my grandson Tyler,
and Stephanie
R. H.

HERE IT WAS, AN EVENING IN LATE AUGUST.

Billy Whee sat on the back steps of his home, elbows on his knees, his hands wrapped around his face, a mason jar at his side. It was at this time of day, sitting in this spot, waiting for his friends to come, with the sun dropping behind the pine forest, a full moon soon to rise, that he awaited the first blink of a lightning bug.

This evening, however, he was a little disappointed. His summer was about to end. Tonight's full moon would be the last of the season. Tomorrow he would start a new school year. He wanted a few more nights like tonight.

Each night Stuart and Juny Layne and Mary Frances Bethel walked from nearby farms, bringing their jars to play a game of catch-the-lightning-bug.

They played as the shadows grew long and slender and the green of the corn stalks turned black as the night grew slowly older.

The old trees in the orchard near the back gate became alive with a full moon.

"Those limbs look like dancers," Mary Frances declared.

"They look like monsters," Juny thought out loud.

"Look like dumb trees," added Stuart.

It was there in the orchard that the lightning bugs first emerged. They had been sleeping in the limbs or the treetops, and all at once the night was filled with flickering bits of light, on and off, circling, flying higher, diving toward the tall grass, sailing sideways, gliding up and down, making giant loops.

"Got the first one," someone would cry.

"Me, too."

"Me, three."

They rushed from bug to bug, stabbing in the dark, hoping to catch one, stumbling over an old log they had seen a million times.

The nights may have seemed the same, but Billy Whee knew that the nights when the moon was full, when it cast shadows over the trees, against the bushes, when it outlined the cows grazing quietly on the other side of the fence, when it skipped along the ruffles of the tin roof on Billy's home—those were the best nights.

They scurried about filling their jars, and soon they were holding glasses with an orange glow, and the glow mingled with the moonlight as the moon floated higher and higher in the sky, moving silently to the west, casting reflections on the windows of the house and making the pond in the distance appear to be a shiny silver dollar.

Suddenly it was nine o'clock. Billy heard the creak of the back screen door, and he knew what was coming. It would be the clear and calm voice of his mother. "Say good night to your friends," she would say. "Come in now, Billy," and, finally, a little firmer: "Now, Billy, now." He was off to bed.

As Billy lay in bed, his eyes were drawn to the window. How could they not be, for the full moon had risen to its peak and it urged its light through his window. I could almost read a book by the light, he thought.

With moonbeams cascading across his room and falling on his white pillow, Billy was restless. He thought, If only I could capture this minute. If only I could put the moon up in the sky whenever I want it.

Billy left his bed. He knelt by the window and stared at the bright, white oval. "If only I could reach out and grab it and pull it inside and put it away and take it out tomorrow night or next week or next month."

With that he reached out. He knew the moon was thousands of miles away, moving in its orbit, silently creeping westward, ready soon to hide for the day behind a cloud in the western sky. He knew that, but his arms stretched farther and farther and soon they touched the moon—the real moon, the bright, white, round moon he had played under all evening. He grabbed it and he felt it firm in his hands and he pulled it toward him. It's coming, it's coming, he thought. He shook with anticipation as the moon was pulled, by his own arms using his own strength, closer and closer to his bedroom window.

It was soon so close he wondered if he had the strength to hold it. He wondered if it might be too large to pull through the window. Finally with one last breath he gave a yank—a yank so determined that something told him that if he had applied that same will in the barn today, he could have tossed hay bales as well as the grown men on the farm had.

And he tumbled backward. He tumbled backward and the moon was in his arms. In his bedroom. Exhausted, he rested, the room now bathed in the exploding light of a full moon.

There on the floor next to the window lay the moon. It was as round as Billy was tall, its surface covered with light and dark dimples. Billy sat on the edge of his bed. He was very tired. Then he heard his mother's footsteps.

"Billy," she said, "turn your lights out and go to sleep."

He started to reply that his lights were not on. Then he realized that what she saw shining beneath his bedroom door was the light of his captured moon. What should he do? He knew that he could not turn it off.

Billy got up, moved to the window, and rolled the moon to his closet. He opened the door, pushed aside his baseball stuff, some books, the box that held his special things, and rolled the moon inside.

He closed the door and climbed back into bed. The moon glowed from beneath the door and through the keyhole. At that moment his mother called again. One word: "Billy!" He knew what that meant.

What next? He tried to fit the moon into a dresser drawer. He pulled out his shirts and underwear, dumping them in a pile on the floor, and gingerly lifted the moon to the open drawer. It would not fit. It stuck out—and the room was as bright as ever.

He looked about, trying to think of a good hiding place. He next tried sliding the moon under his bed. That did no good. His room was as bright as morning. He thought about putting it under his bedsheets, but where would he sleep?

He looked for more places to hide the moon. He had an idea. He pulled two chairs together and made a tent of his sheet and rolled the moon beneath it. But the moonlight was barely dimmed. Where else? he thought. But there were no other hiding places.

It was past ten o'clock. His mother would soon walk in. What if she saw the moon?

He had to put the moon back where he had found it. He had to roll it to the window, lift it up again, put it back on its path across the sky.

As Billy lifted the moon to the windowsill, it seemed even heavier than before. It seemed brighter, too. Billy squinted as he tried to lift the moon. Suddenly, he lost his grip and the moon slipped from his grasp and fell out of his window.

He watched in horror as the moon hit the ground beneath his window.

It landed and began to roll.

The moon rolled across the yard, through a flower bed; miraculously it headed for and went right through the back gate, into the cornfield between two rows, and disappeared over a hill and out of sight.

Billy fell asleep until he heard his mother's call in the morning. Sleepily he sat at the kitchen table and ate his breakfast. His father walked outside, but soon he was back in the kitchen.

"Under Billy's window," he said, "there is a deep hole—an impression, one might call it. And from there, there is a path across the yard, even over Mother's flower bed, through the back gate, through the corn, and apparently over the hill near the pond. Never seen anything like it."

"I know what it is," Billy said.

"Billy," his mother said, "it's time to catch the school bus."

"But I know—"

"Billy!"

He finished his cereal.

He wanted to share his secret with his friends at school. But it occurred to him: they'll never believe me. Not Mother or Dad. Not Juny or Stuart or Mary Frances. It would sound like one of Mary Frances's exaggerated tales. The very idea. The very idea of a ten year old reaching out, capturing the moon. It was a dream, someone would say.

As he waited for the bus to arrive, his mind turned to the fading days of August and the elusive moon. This summer would soon be over, but there would be next summer and the summer after, and the moon would return again and again. It would make its own way, follow its own path, a sliver, a quarter, a half—finally full.

And there would still be tonight. Stuart and Juny and Mary Frances would come one last time before evenings would be consumed with schoolwork. It would be a good night—a night for lightning bugs under a moon he once held in his arms.